Chère Jocelyne,
un tout petit quelque chose
pour te transmettre mon énor.
et aussi pour souhaiter "bonheur"
à ta grande famille ...

Olga.
10.07. '84

*By the same authors*

Alistair in Outer Space

# ALISTAIR'S ELEPHANT

by Marilyn Sadler

Illustrated by Roger Bollen

Hamish Hamilton · London

Alistair Grittle was a very busy boy.
He had no time for nonsense.

He worked very hard at school. When he knew the answer to a question, he would raise both of his hands.

He was very neat and tidy. He cleaned his room
every night and slept on top of his covers.

Alistair also found time to play. He was very careful to choose games that exercised his mind as well as his body.

Every Saturday Alistair went to the zoo because that was the day they offered a special admission rate for children under ten. Alistair was thrifty too.

On Saturday, when Alistair was going to the zoo,
it threatened rain. So Alistair took an umbrella.

When he got to the zoo, he decided which animals
he most wanted to see. Then he studied his zoo

map, walked quickly, and stopped only once for a
chocolate bar too small to spoil his dinner.

He set out for home only after he had thanked the zoo keeper for a most enjoyable afternoon.

When it began to rain, Alistair was glad he had taken his umbrella.

He was nearly home when he realized something quite surprising. He was being followed by an elephant.

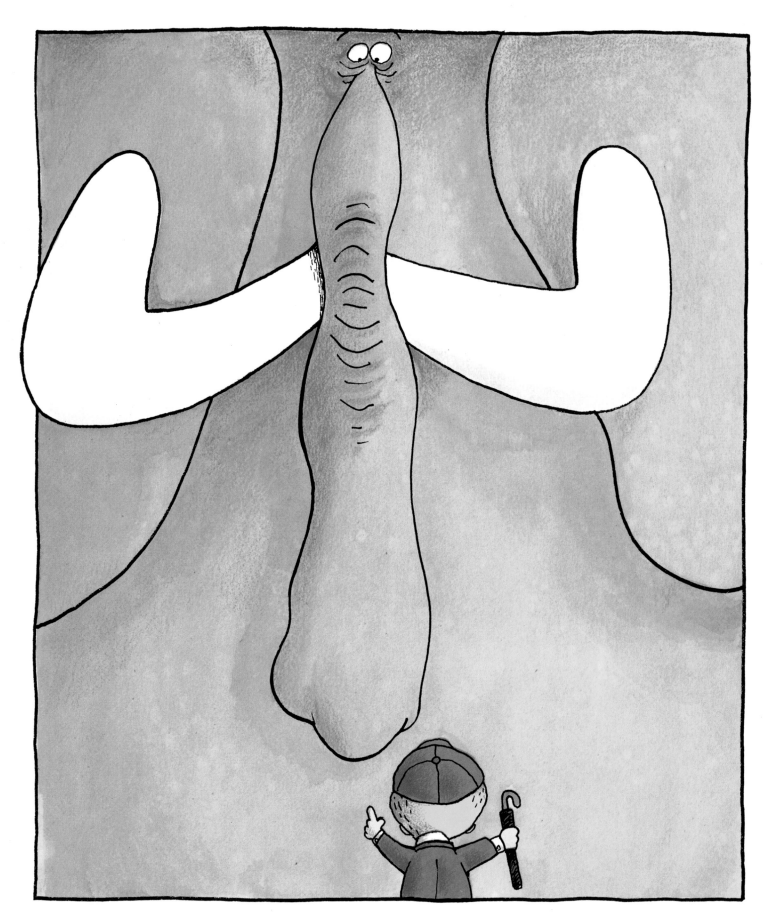

"The zoo keeper will be very worried about you!" cried Alistair. "You must go back to the zoo!" But the elephant wouldn't go.

Alistair was late for dinner, so there was nothing
he could do but let the elephant follow him home.

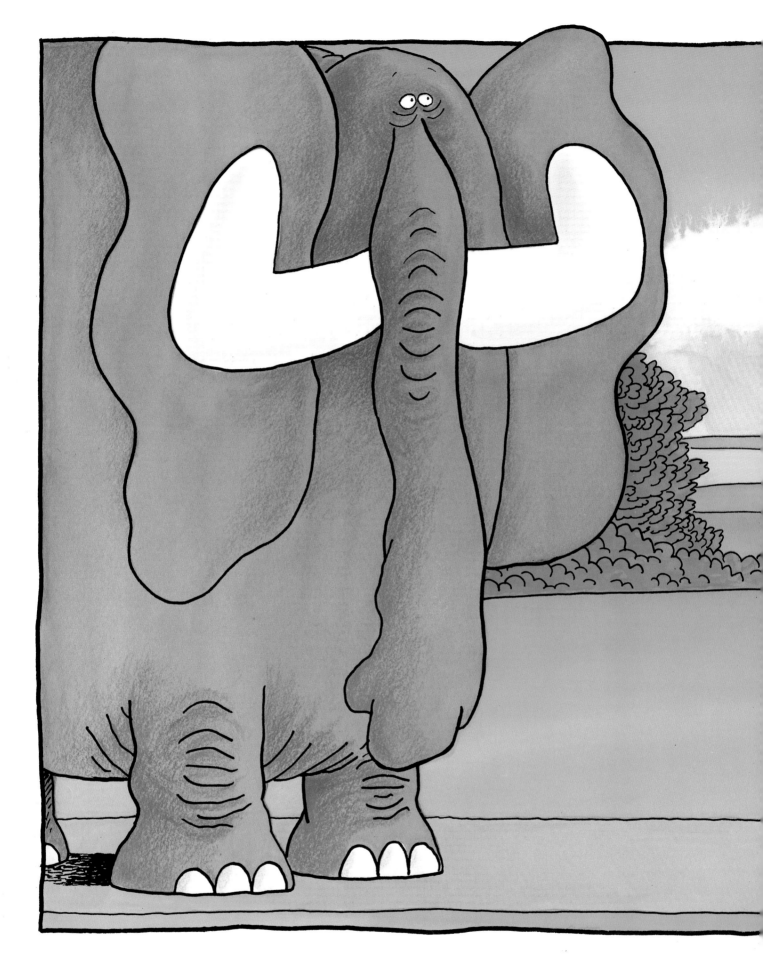

"You can't keep him!" shouted his mother from the window. Alistair didn't want to. He didn't have time for a pet.

So he called the zoo keeper and the
zoo keeper checked his records.
There was a hippopotamus missing,
but not an elephant. "Are you sure
it's not a hippo?" he asked. Alistair
was certain.

There was nothing Alistair could do but eat his dinner and hope that the elephant would leave. He was so upset, he couldn't eat his favourite vegetables.

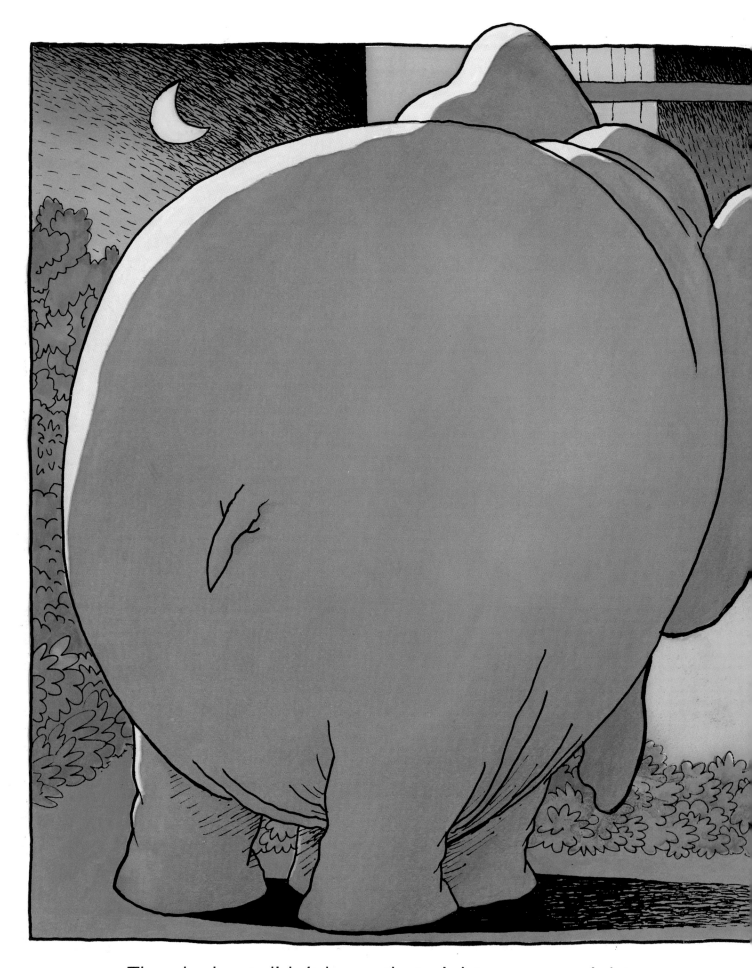

The elephant didn't leave that night, nor any night that week. Alistair had a very hard time sleeping with the elephant at his window.

Even though Alistair got up early, the elephant got up earlier.

Alistair didn't have any privacy. He had to dress in the cupboard.

The elephant followed him to school and caused so much excitement that everyone had to be sent home. Alistair did not get to take the arithmetic test he had studied so hard for.

The elephant ate all of Alistair's house plants, as well as his science book and his stamp collection.

Alistair tried to teach the elephant how to behave.
The elephant did get a little better and even gave
Alistair some privacy.

On school days the elephant learned
to stay at home.

On Saturday, however, Alistair took the elephant back to the zoo. He just didn't have time for an elephant every day of the week.

The zoo keeper checked his records
again and found a mistake. He had
been missing an elephant after all.
He thanked Alistair very much.

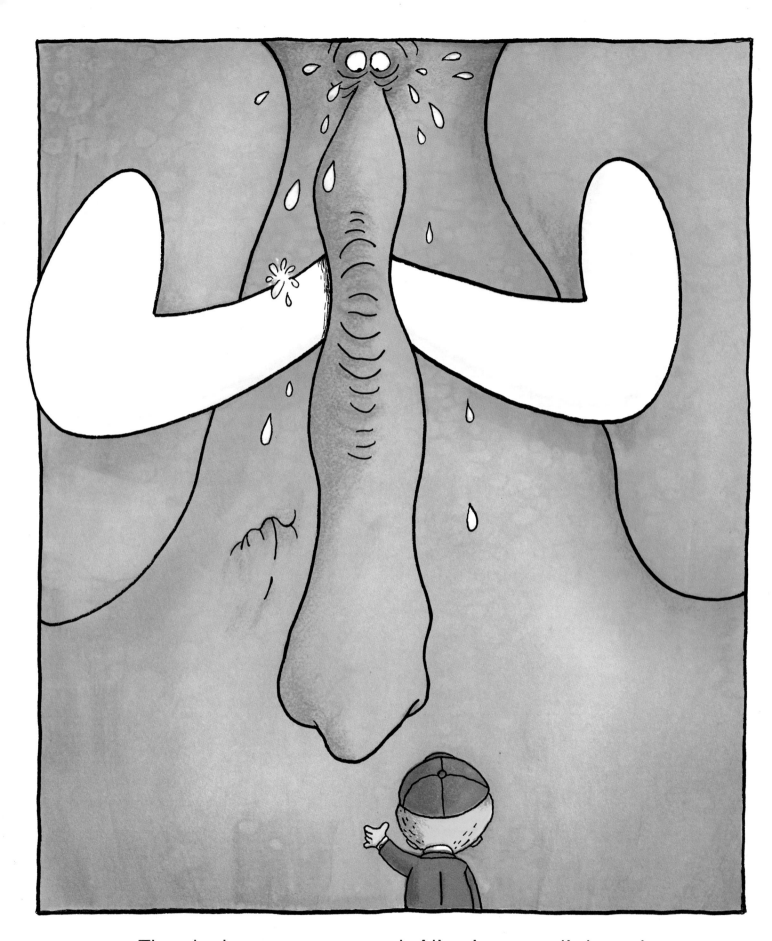

The elephant was very sad. Alistair was a little sad too, but he promised the elephant he would visit every Saturday.

Then Alistair left for home. It had been a busier week than usual and, at times, it had been fun. But he was very happy to be going home to his quiet, tidy room where, at last...

...he could get some work done.

First Published in 1983
Published by Hamish Hamilton Children's Books
Garden House, 57-59 Long Acre, London WC2E 9JZ
Copyright © 1983 by Roger Bollen and Marilyn Sadler
Reprinted 1984
All rights reserved
British Library Cataloguing in Publication Data
Alistair's elephant
Bollen, Roger
I. Title
II. Sadler, Marilyn
823'.914[J] PZj
ISBN 0-241-10809-8
Printed in Belgium by
Henri Proost & Cie